A Bus Ride for One

Rosie Siderova

Copyright © 2019 by Rosie Siderova

Cover Design: *Rebecacovers*

Edit and Proofread: *Flora Brown*

This is a work of fiction.

Names, characters, places, and incidents are the product of the author's imagination or are used fictiously, and any resemblance to actual persons, living or dead, businesses, companies, events, or locales is entirely coincidental.

This book is meant to make your afternoon even more pleasant. Along with a cup of coffee, made just as you like it.

Smiles.

"A bus ride for one" is dedicated to all those people who for whatever reason had to face a loss of a loved one.

 Now they are here, standing proudly with their heads up, stronger than ever and ready to love even more. Because the game called life will never stop and we are its players forever.

With love,

Rosie

Table of Contents

Lolla

She heard her mom's voice calling her from the kitchen downstairs, but her mind was elsewhere. Staring at the old picture, she slowly ran her fingers through the green frame. She was thinking of those exact days, precisely a year ago. It seemed like it was just yesterday and they were happy. Her thoughts were chaotic – they were angry, and then they were sad, and this circle seemed like it was never going to end.

She felt the anger; that familiar feeling has been following her throughout her days since then, and it seemed like there was nothing else to be done. She used to fight it; she was refusing to accept the truth, but she gave up with the months. Her days turned into loneliness.

A text message notification brought her back to reality, and she reached for her phone. It was Patty asking her if she would like to go to a yoga class with her. She thought for a second; it has been so long since last time, she remembered. "Why not!" Lolla said to herself surprisingly. She had an hour to get herself together and find those yoga pants she lost months ago with the moving. This was going to be interesting.

Lolla went downstairs and looked at her mom standing so beautiful and making dinner for all of them. She adored her mother since she was a little girl and always wanted to be like her when she grows up, always telling all her friends how cool of a mom she had. Something so rare, especially for a twenty-two-year-old girl. Diana looked at Lolla and smiled instantly.

"Sweetie, how are you? Come on, sit down and let's talk, I will make you some tea," her mom said and hugged her tightly.

Lolla burst into tears - every time she feels her mom's love and energy, she could not hold it. They were best friends, and they became so exactly a year ago.

The kitchen was small and bright. There was so much more to be done but her mom was tired. She worked as a travel agent in a big company and her days were filled with work. Lolla loved her mom's taste; everything was simple, organized, and so color coordinated. Lolla used to help her mother with everything around the house – colors, furniture, and all kinds of designs.

It has been quite a while now since the last time Lolla showed any interest about the house or the kitchen. Now she wasn't interested in anything.

She moved with her family from Ohio to Boston a couple of years ago, and it was a big change for all of them. Lola's mom was promoted at her job and had a great opportunity to run her own travel agency. This was something that does not happen to everyone every day. So they decided to go ahead and make that move. Boston seemed like a great adventure – full of opportunities and life.

Her parents chose a house that was owned by a bank. The place was huge, and it was in a great location, just a couple of minutes from the subway. The house needed so much work inside and outside. Even when Lolla first saw the house, she said that it looks like a house from a Horror movie. However, her dad was a very handy man, and besides his wine, he loved doing everything around the house. And little by little, it was all coming together for all of them.

Until exactly a year ago.

Lolla kissed her mom and reached for her backpack, slowly walking away.

"Thank you, mom, I will do a Yoga class in a bit and will join you all for dinner," Lolla quietly said to her mom. "I need to start my life from somewhere. By the way, I am excited to see my new classmates."She grabbed her mat and a bottle of cold water and blew a kiss to her mom.

Diana sat on the kitchen table and thought of Lolla when she was a little girl - she would always make jokes, like funny jokes; her little face covered in freckles and Nutella.

"Wow, what a blessing," she whispered to herself. Diana looked at the boiling pasta and started laughing. If Lolla had seen what was actually boiling, she would have said, "Mom, you are the best - thank you for making pasta all these three days in a row." Yes, another one of her clever jokes. However, that would have also happened a year ago, Lolla was not so much into jokes since then.

The yoga class

olla entered the yoga room and looked at her bare feet. It has been so long since she felt the cold, hardwood floor under her toes. She moved them around and smiled. Patty was standing right next to her and thinking how beautiful her friend is, and she felt so glad that they are here together again. There was so much love in the air - the calmness, compassion, and gratitude. They put their mats right next to each other and smiled. The class was about to begin, and everyone was slowing down in moves, getting ready to relax the mind and stretch their physical bodies. The daily routine of life was left behind the closed doors.

A light meditation music was coming from a concealed speaker while the teacher was walking around the hall lighting up small candles. The lavender and sandalwood scent filled the entire air.

"Welcome everyone and Namaste."The teacher sat on her mat in front of everyone, she was smiling and taking deep breathes. Her name was Toni, and she has been teaching this class for years. Her blonde hair was tied, and her body was in incredible shape. Her face radiated good and tranquility. She was preparing the group for the session. "Let all of us take a couple of deep breaths and just let go of all stress, negativity, and pain." She was speaking quietly and smiling while closing her eyes.

Her voice was soothing and calming, and Lolla realized that she has been missing yoga so much. Her breathing started to slow down, and her body felt light. Every pose came natural and with ease. She wondered how incredible the human body is, and after a year of not practicing, the flexibility and calmness were still there. They say that the body remembers – just like you can't forget how to drive a car or ride a bike. Perhaps her body had pitied her.

"It must be that," she smiled. "And I feel so grateful."

Her favorite time in yoga class has come - final relaxation and meditation. She remembered there was nothing like this amazing feeling of happiness and joy she used to feel back then. It has been so long, exactly a year ago. She wondered if she will be able to experience it now, even something similar to what it was before. *It takes time, it takes a practice,* she thought, *but it's all worth it.*

She shook her head; she was thinking too much, and it wasn't the time now, it wasn't the place either. Patty was glancing at her friend from time to time, making sure her best friend is doing okay. It was almost unbelievable –two of them, together, right now.

Yes, way too much thinking, let me just breathe and relax, Lolla though. She moved her hands and legs and tried to get more comfortable on the mat.

Everyone lay down on their mats, and the teacher started reading a part of a wonderful book. It was all about the spiritual health of every human, a true belief that every soul is immortal, and that love is all.

The small lights that came from the candles around them glittered before her eyes as if they were playing a fairy tale. Her eyelids felt heavy,and she knew that the long-awaited moment has arrived. She was going to be happy again.

A strange feeling started from her toes and reached her ankles and knees. It was not exactly tickling or tingling, but something very light and enjoyable. She felt a giant cold wave pass through her body, and the feeling was extraordinary. The deep relaxing moment had her melt away in her mat ,and she fell asleep with a huge smile on her face.

Colin

Colin grabbed her hand and they started running towards the little house at the end of the valley. She couldn't see his face clearly, but she knew it's him. Lolla was wearing her baby blue dress that she bought from a little boutique years ago. *How am I wearing this dress since mommy shrank it in the dryer last year?* she thought, but didn't have time to ponder on it. Colin ran ahead of her, and she was trying to catch up with him. Where is he hurrying to like that? Her mind was racing with so many questions and thoughts and she was in shock.

What is happening? How is this possible? But why do I feel so happy? Lolla felt tired and exhausted, she could no longer continue. She tried to stop him and to slow down, but for some reason this seemed impossible.

They started to approach and he stuck the step. He was still walking in front of her without turning his head but still held her hand firmly. The entire house was made of light brown wood, and it had two yellow chairs on the porch. It seemed like a fairy tale, and they were quick to get involved as actors.In front of the porch, there were planted flowers, and many butterflies flew past them. Colin turned and smiled with his whole face to Lolla. She was shaking and couldn't breathe from the run. She stared at his face. His hair was jet black, his teeth were white, and his skin was glowing. Colin's eyes were full of joy, and Lolla was blinking and rubbing her own eyes, trying to understand what was happening.

"What is this Colin, what is going on?"She hugged him firmly and felt the familiar smell of his skin. She had not felt it for so long, and her tears started trickling down her cheeks.

"This is my surprise for you, my love. I have been waiting for you," he said and wrung his fingers in her hair.

"But...you are gone," she said."This is impossible, am I gone too?"

"No, my love, you are not gone, our love is still so strong. You need to feel peace and calmness so that I can come to you. Every time you feel this feeling, I will be here for you waiting," Colin smiled and kissed her hand.

The last time he kissed her hand was exactly a year ago.

A dream?

They sat in the two chairs and stared straight into each other's eyes. Colin was so handsome. His presence wiped out all of the traces of sadness and despair that had stood in her heart. He smiled and caressed her hand. Gradually, his silhouette began to move away and the bright sunlight began to cover everything. Colin was still smiling at her, but now she was seeing him in a distance,and his appearance was going further and further. Lolla tried to hold his hand tightly, but an invisible force separated them. A sense of indescribable sadness began to sneak into her heart, black as a dark winter night. Was she losing him again, and why?

Lolla was lying down on her mat still with her eyes closed. She was smiling. The whispering voice of the teacher who finished the meditation reached her.

"Thank you, everyone. That was an amazing class, and I will see you all next Thursday, at6 pm. All of you be healthy, good, and humble. Namaste."

She heard Patty getting up from her mat and walking away towards the dressing rooms.

"How good was this class, baby!?" Patty was yelling at her. "Next Thursday again!"

Lolla took a deep breath and started opening her eyes slowly; she could still feel his hand holding on to hers. And his lips on her hand. She looked at the ceiling and thought it looked just like the blackboards they used to have in school, dark and covered with smudged chalk writings. She focused her sight on one of the inspirational quotes written among the others "Ask, believe, receive."She smiled, *it sounds so simple and beautiful,* she thought. "Can I ask for this dream again? I would do anything to see Colin again." She moved her legs and arms and sat down on the mat. For the first time in a long time, the hard rock she had in her throat seemed to have disappeared. She could breathe easily. She looked at her bare feet and moved her toes a bit, and they seemed to know the dance of love.

Wine and Love

Diana opened the wine fridge and started to look at the wine bottles. She grabbed the Merlot and opened it. Its label seemed like the coolest one, and the Italian wines were her favorite also .She never liked red wine, especially when she tried a little sip out of her dad's glass when she was only four.This was Martin's nightmare; he never had a company for a bottle of wine. However, this changed drastically when he surprised her with a vacation to Napa Valley in California for their second wedding anniversary. It was incredible. They visited so many local wineries, and by the end of the trip, Diana felt like a wine expert herself. That is when she found out about the existence of the Merlot, and it became her favorite. She was enjoying it daily since then. And of course, Martin was the happiest of all; now he had a wine partner as well.

Martin was a huge wine lover, he was born in a family of winemakers, famous for their products for centuries. His dad was making his own wine back in Bulgaria, and Martin was always there to help him. When he turned fifteen years old, he was given an opportunity to pick and mix a variety of grapes. They produced a rich and flavorful red wine. It was the first wine he produced, and his family was extremely proud of him. The passion continued with the years and even increased when Martin and his dad went to a wine competition in the capital and won second place. Martin carefully chose the grapes they used to make the wine for the competition. His dad trusted him and knew that Martin has a great intuition, so he decided to go with his son's choice, which turned out to be an excellent choice.

Within the years, Martin continued his passion and became one of the best winemakers in Eastern Europe. And that's how he met Diana. It was definitely not love on the first sight, but it was love.

She was sitting on a brown little chair sipping a glass of red wine. From her facial expression, he knew this is not her favorite, but she was still proudly holding on the glass. Martin thought she looked adorable and wondered why she was there.

"May I ask, what kind are you sipping?" he approached with a smile.

"A red one," she said and looked down at her glass with a smirk.

"I see, but what kind and what is the winery that makes it?" he laughed.

"Not sure," she responded and smelled the wine in her glass."I guess a good one; my dad poured me some and left me over here alone," she explained.

"I see," Martin said, "well, let me introduce myself. My name is Martin, and I come from Bulgaria, I am a winemaker, continuing my family business and here is my winery booth over here," he pointed to a bright red booth in the end of the hall which she thought was pretty small but very cute.

"Well, Martin, my name is Diana, and I am from Ohio, USA. My dad and I came to California for this wine seminar and tasting together, he is also a winemaker, but unfortunately, I am not a wine fan. However, I decided to join him so he is not by himself and I love to travel. It is my first time here," she explained.

"Well, I cannot be happier," he said, "now we met each other, and we can just try different kinds of wine together. I will enjoy my wine, and you will just make funny faces on the side."

They both laughed and tried some really good wines from all over the world.They spent some really good time together. Two years later, he moved to the states and married her.

Wine

Diana sipped on the Merlot and closed her eyes; it was blissful. No other drink would make her feel so happy. She always joked around that she wasted so many years of her life without enjoying wine. Many wasted years.This was the truth.

She heard the door open and put down the glass on her counter. Martin was taking his coat off and was all smiling.

"It smells delicious in here," he said.

"I made pasta again," she laughed and kissed him.

"I meant, the Merlot, babe." Martin raised his eyebrows and smiled.

They both laughed, like always. Their relationship was based on so much love and fun, even in times of sad moments, money issues or anything else, they always made each other laugh. Nothing was 'way too serious' to be a real problem.

"Where is Lolla?"he said, "I thought we are all going to have dinner together finally."

"She is coming, babe," Diana answered, "she went to a yoga class with Patty. Can you imagine? I almost couldn't believe my eyes when I saw her today all dressed in her yoga pants, holding her mat proudly."

Martin looked surprised and smiled, that was one wonderful thing. She has not been to a yoga class in exactly one year. *Were things slowly getting back to normal? It should be like that, right? Sooner or later, people heal,* he thought.

"Yes, do not look like this is something bad, Martin, it is progress," Diana said. His face was looking serious and somehow sad.

"Absolutely and no, definitely not a bad thing at all. Just waiting for you to pour me a glass of this wine, babe, that is what my face is saying," he laughed.

Let me tell you something

The street looked so peaceful and quiet; all brightened from the street lighting. The summer was coming to an end and the nights were getting longer. Lolla felt the little breeze on her cheeks when she left the yoga center.

"You are always cold, my dear, even after sweating in a yoga class, how is this even possible?" Patty said to her while making a funny face.

"My body is cold but my heart is warm!" Lolla answered and stood straight and tall.

They both laughed and hugged each other. It has been quite a while since they did anything together. Patty's heart was overflowing with love for Lolla, seeing her best friend happy and definitely better.

The past year has been rough, like really rough. They say a real friendship can go through anything, but there are some really wild examples out there of what exactly friends could go through. You would always think that people who know each other for the longest, stay best friends forever. Is it really that way? Or maybe someone enters your life, and the person becomes so close to your heart that you just do not remember life before them. Whatever it is, when it is meant to be, it will always be.

Patty was standing in front of Lolla, looking at her face and a million thoughts were racing in her mind. Lolla was her sister – not like blood sister but someone she adored from the first moment they met each other.

Patty and Lolla were both seven years old. They were in Mexico with their families at the same time, at the same resort. It was January of 1993,and it was their first time being out of the United States. Patty was "scanning" the breakfast buffet very carefully one morning when Lolla approached her and said, "I hope they do not make boiled eggs here! It is Mexico after all!" she said and crossed her arms.

"I am sure they do, everything is very Americanized as I see," answered Patty very serious.

Lolla stared at her and turned her back. What a rude girl, she thought. Maybe she should go back to the States and eat her eggs there.

"FYI I am not a fan of them either," Patty yielded to her.

Lolla turned her head around ,and they smiled at each other. This was it – fourteen years later, they were still best friends and still hated boiled eggs.

-"Listen, I have to tell you something," Lolla said, "something serious, Pat."

Patty looked at her and made a surprised face. She would always say 'something serious' when she meant really something serious. Her stomach tightened and she felt fear. She was finally getting her best friend back, and she wasn't sure if she wanted to hear what Lolla has to say. Or if she was ready to hear anything serious.

"Miss Lolla," Patty pointed a finger at her, "are you trying to tell me you didn't enjoy Ms. Clarison's class? I saw you fall asleep which was funny, but I still love you," Patty tried to joke around. She wanted to escape what was coming.

"No, Pat. I enjoyed it, actually way too much. But, listen, I know you will think I'm crazy and not normal or whatever, but I have to tell you – I saw Colin."

They both stood on the street in silence. Patty held on to her hand, and it seemed like she wanted to speak, but there were no words. It was shocking and insane. It was also not possible. And it was really scary.

"Oh honey, did you dream of him? That is so wonderful, I dream of my grandmom all the time, this is a way they remind us they are watching over us."

"No, Pat, you are not listening to me. I saw him. I felt him; I talked to him, we were together but not here in this physical world. However, it was real. Real like you and me right now, right here."

"How, when? I don't understand." Patty stepped back and held her head like she was trying to ease a headache. "You are scaring me, and you need to tell your mom, maybe you need to talk to someone. Not sure, maybe a doctor, I will come with you."

Lolla smiled and stepped towards Patty; she hugged her and told her that everything is okay. At the end of the day, it did sound like something that can't be real. She got angry at herself for not thinking this through better; she should have waited and shared it with Patty in a better way. However, it was so amazing, and she wanted to share it with her best friend. It was Colin, and it was not a dream.

Patty hugged Lolla back; she was worried.

She knew

L olla turned on her car and looked herself in the mirror. She could still feel Colin's presence around her. She took her phone out of her bag and typed the website of the yoga studio; she needed to come back as soon as possible. She instantly believed the meditation at the end of the class brought Colin back to her. There it was – next Tuesday at 6pm. She was so happy and dialed Patty's number, and they arranged another yoga class date together. All she could think about was Colin.

Her life has changed so much since he was gone. It was the most unfair accident that changed her life forever. And she will never be able to get used to it. For someone like Lolla – young and free, full of life and so much in love For The First Time, this was a true stop. Just like when you hit the Pause button on the remote and the scene on the screen freezes. People are still there, but the thoughts, the moves, and the music are all gone. It is only you, and you are alone. Also it's quiet, you feel your heart beating, and you keep breathing. Cold stone is stuck in your chest and is making your breathing hard, and all you can do is to wait until it all passes. Is it ever going to pass? You have to manage and reach the remote and click the Play button again.

Thoughts were racing through her mind, and this has been her reality for a whole year. School became just a place she goes every morning and sit on the chair, just being there. You are just a body. Everything that was happening was unfair.

What was supposed to be normal for someone her age was not what was normal for her after that day.

You listen to people telling you that everything will be okay, but you know deep down that this is never going to happen. So you just wait. You go through your daily routine after putting a mask on your face because you have a family and friends who are trying to make everything better for you and you do not want to hurt them. All you actually need is to be under your covers and to be left alone. Or until your forever decides it's time for you to hit the Play button again and be alive. The movie continues.

There was only Silence.

This was all her life until thirty minutes ago when she saw him, and the cold stone in her chest melted. And she knew he was back – not for the world, but for her. Because when you believe it is love, then it is love. She was patiently waiting for the miracle, and the miracle happened.

Lolla smiled. And she felt that for the first time in a while she was hungry.

Hey, family

She walked into her house and smelled the pasta. This instantly made her happy – it was her favorite thing. Martin's face looked so surprised – Lolla was glowing.Little warm tears started to fall down his face, and it was really hard for him to try to cover them. He was trying to hide them, but his voice was showing his excitement.

"Lolla!"he said."Hi! What is going on, sweety?"He got up and ran to hug her. Something has changed, and he could feel it with his entire being. Even the air around her was different. There was hope around.

"Hey dad," Lolla replied with a huge smile, returning the huge, warm hug he was giving her."I am good! Let's eat, and please can I also have some wine?"

"Of course!"he said."This yoga class must have been phenomenal, you are different! Can I join you next time, please?" he laughed. "And where is Patty?"

"She went back home, her mom is not feeling okay again, "Lolla said. "But yes, the class was awesome, going next week again." Lolla started to wash her hands on the sink, looking for one of those really pretty wine glasses her aunt Tanya got for her mom's Birthday last year.

Diana heard the door opening downstairs and hurried to finish folding the laundry. She must have come home, and I should go and start the dinner table, she thought. I pray for a nice night and conversations, one family dinner, she smiled in the mirror, folding Lolla's favorite pajamas.

Ever since Colin passed, Lolla changed. It was normal and anyone could have been the same way, but seeing her daughter losing her fate in life was the most painful thing she ever had to go through. Not even when Diana lost her parents – no one lives forever, right? But it was different – his death was a shock to everyone, and he left this world so young and full of life. It was unfair, it was wrong. Now Lolla was just existing – not interested in anything, not leaving the house, not caring for the future. Nothing and no one seemed to help her in any way.

Diana's heart was broken into pieces, but she knew she has to stay strong and keep believing because that's what a mother is supposed to do. And Lolla was her world. There were millions of sleepless nights, full of tears and a broken heart of a mother, but this all stayed hidden from Lolla. Her only escape was her job, and sometimes even Martin was getting angry saying that she loves her job more than him. But that was her only true distraction.

For a hot second, they thought there was light in the tunnel when the school psychologist took Lolla under his wing, and it seemed like there was a little progress. For all of the eight months she was seeing him, Lolla was trying. The truth was that deep down, she knew this was not helping her, but she felt like she needs to give it a shot because of her parents. She saw the hope in their eyes and tried to pretend that things were working. But they weren't. So after a while, she admitted it's a waste of money. She didn't want to listen to anybody because no one could ever convince her that there was a logical explanation of what had happened.

Martin and Diana searched the entire country, hoping to find someone who could really help her. Everything was always ending with "Time will heal."

She hugged the pajamas and smelled it; it was reminding her of the times when Lolla was a little girl, not wanting to take off her pajamas ever and would wear it an entire day. Diana smiled. *Such precious memories,* she thought.

It was time for some pasta and wine. Diana went down the stairs and stood on the last stair shocked. Lolla was sitting right by her dad on a high chair and had the biggest smile on her face, holding a glass of red wine. She pinched her skin to make sure she was not dreaming. Last time she saw this beautiful smile was exactly a year ago.

It's next Thursday

Lolla opened her eyes and smiled. It was a sunny morning, and the sun was peeking in the room through the shades. She had a plan for today – she wanted to take care of herself, it has been so long since she has done that. She decided to call for a hair appointment and to check if maybe they have an opening for her today. She wanted her hair blonder. There was a small nail salon next to her hairdresser, so she decided to visit it as well. She wanted to look stunning for him tonight. She got up and started to look for her phone – her old friend Nona had texted her if she wants to grab a bite and catch up. They were old friends and met back in the kindergarten. Lolla didn't remember the last time they saw each other, but she felt so happy and responded right away to arrange dinner plans.

Lolla put on her pink sweats and went downstairs. She immediately smelled the French toast. This was her all-time favorite breakfast. Diana was sitting on the countertop, sipping on her freshly brewed coffee.

"Good morning, mom, what you got for me?" Lolla smiled."I want some coffee too. I need some more energy for today, have so much to do!"

Diana hugged her daughter and smiled. She still could not believe what has happened to Lolla, so she returned to herself so quickly. She was looking absolutely beautiful.

Maybe she has met someone? For a week now she was wondering and trying to figure out the reason behind her sudden change, but at the end of the day, she was truly happy. Lolla has come back.

"Oh, yeah? And what is so important about your plans, missy?" Diana smiled."I missed this beautiful smile of yours."She was touching Lolla's hair and started to brush it.

Lolla's hair was beautiful, long down to her lower back, blonde, curly, and shiny. It has been so long since she had her hair down, she would always have it up in a bun or a pony tail. *She would always be absolutely beautiful*, Diana thought.

"I have the yoga class today, remember?" Lolla smiled. I am going to get a haircut and do my nails; it's been so long, mom."

Diana sipped her coffee and grabbed her phone. She found her text conversations with Martin and typed, "Babe, I am sure, she must have met someone at the yoga class, she is going to do her hair and nails today before class!!!"

Lolla enjoyed her breakfast and coffee while they talked about the house. They made a plan to go out on the weekend and maybe pick a new dining set and can surprise Martin afterward with it. She changed her sweats to her favorite jeans, grabbed her car keys and left the house, whispering a Christmas song.

"Yesss!" Martin responded.

36

A second dream maybe

"**N**amaste, everyone! And let's begin!"

Toni's voice was so mild and was bringing calmness to the room. Lolla felt her heart beating so quickly, she couldn't hold her breath, and she felt as if she was about to cry. She has been waiting for this moment for a whole week, knowing she will meet him again. This thought was giving her the strength to get up every morning and continue with her life. She felt the energy flowing through her shivering body, and there it was - amazing peace and light.

While lying down on her mat, she realized that this past week was different, she was coming back to the life slowly. She was so used to the dark, and her days were spent in tears and loneliness. Being only twenty-two, this seemed to be nothing but a huge mess, the wrong turn you take at a crossroad. However, it was real, and it was her life now.

Lolla smiled – everything was starting to change, Colin has come back, and she was about to see him again in one, two, three deep breathes.

It's him and I again

Lolla opened her eyes and looked around. She felt the cold breeze playing with her hair. Her bare feet were hanging from the rock, and for the first time, she didn't feel the fear of heights. She couldn't see how deep this dark gap is but she knew she was safe. She found herself sitting on its edge, holding a picture of her and Colin in her right hand. She looked at his face – he was so handsome. She remembered this moment back then. It was when they decided to cook together for the first time. Well, in the end, the chicken was over roasted and the potatoes needed more boiling. Colin took that picture of them holding their empty stomachs. It was such a fun night. Lolla smiled and held the picture to her heart. *The pizza we ordered afterward was also very tasty*, she thought.

But where was he right now?

She listened to the wind and felt the cold; it was coming from the gap in front of her, the rock she was sitting on was freezing. She closed her eyes and smiled. It was happening again.

"Hey there."She heard Colin's voice."Sorry I am late!"

"Colin!" Lolla jumped immediately and started running towards him. Tears started coming down her face, and she started feeling warmer and warmer.

Colin was standing with his arms wide open, waiting to hug her. Nothing has changed; his eyes were so bright, and his smile was bigger than the world. Lolla hugged him so strongly and said, "Can you come home with me? I have so much to share with you. We need to continue this life together, I can't do it by myself, Colin."

"Hey, don't cry."Colin tried to wipe her tears off her face. "I am here, and I will always be here for you. Now calm down, I want to show you something," he said and grabbed her hand.

They started to walk slowly, still holding hands. It was just like a year ago on a summer night when they walked down her house after an afternoon spent in the park. She remembered that he stopped and turned his head to her, asking her to close her eyes.

Lolla started laughing and joking if there will be a ring involved. Colin was very serious and made her spin around her body a couple of times. She was laughing and spinning at the same time and was joking that she will feel very dizzy after she stops. And then it would be very hard for him to put the ring on her finger. It was such a fun emotion, and it was unforgettable.

"Okay, now you can open your eyes, babe," she heard him but she didn't want to open her eyes, she wanted to feel this forever, a moment of surprise and knowing that someone has thought of you and wanted to make you happy. Lolla opened her eyes finally and screamed:

"Omg!" Lolla screamed and started jumping."It's a bicycle!"

Lolla never learned to ride a bicycle. When she was a little girl, her grandpa brought her a really nice one from Russia where he was serving in the army, but she never actually learned how to ride it. She would always be afraid and would just look at it in the corner of the closet. The little red bicycle was still there.

"Now, my love, you have no excuses but to learn how to ride it. Yes, a little late but better later than never."

This was one of the best days of her life.

Lolla was smiling, she thought of this moment back in the day and looked at Colin's face. He was such a wonderful boy, so caring, so thoughtful.

Colin looked back at her and said, "I am angry you actually never learned how to ride it, so make sure you do that by next week when we meet," he juggled.

"How did you know what I am thinking?!" Lolla was shocked. She didn't even say a word about her bike.

"I just know it all," he smiled.

"You are amazing," she said ,"now tell me, where are you taking me?"

"You will see, my love, be patient." Colin kept walking and looking at his watch.

Time exists in here too, that is crazy, Lolla was thinking to herself. *I don't even know where we are, but there is time, mm okay.*

The dinner

Lolla realized she was wearing her green heels. They were her favorite. Diana got them for her when she was turning sixteen. A couple of moments ago, she was bare feet, sitting on the rock alone and didn't remember putting them on. She smiled. Some good things can't be explained, and there is nothing wrong with that. Her heart was the happiest, and she was right here walking right next to him.

"Now close your eyes, love, it's time." Colin turned to her and kissed her lips.

"Okay, I am ready, always and forever ready, Colin." Lolla took a deep breath and closed her eyes.

She started to hear low music, something Italian and she was hearing lots of voices and conversations. She was still holding on to his hand, but it felt different, she felt warm waves coming to her face and she heard a door opening. She opened her eyes slowly and saw they were standing in front of a beautiful restaurant. There was a huge fireplace in the corners, and the whole place was decorated with pictures of sunflowers. They walked in and were greeted by the hostess who was holding a bottle of wine. Colin smiled and said, "We have a reservation under Miss Lolla Smith."

"Yes, sir, welcome," the hostess said and smiled. "The rest of the party is already here, please follow me."

Lolla was so shocked.*The rest of the party?!Who else could have been here ?*She didn't even know where she was.

They passed by many tables; people were laughing and having a great time, everyone was cheering and enjoying themselves. Lolla felt instantly happy, there was a feeling of peace and so much love at this place.

"Here is your table, miss, hope you will have a wonderful time," the hostess smiled and stepped away.

They were two people already sitting there, smiling, with tears in their eyes. Lolla stood in front of the table and felt like her blood was boiling, her heart was beating fast, and she felt she is about to faint. The couple stood up and went to hug her. Lolla smiled and hugged them back strongly. "I have missed you so much, we have so much to talk," Lolla said.

The rest of the party was her grandparents who left the physical world years ago. The night was unbelievable, just like the good old times, Lolla couldn't wait to go home and tell her parents, but she knew no one would have believed her. Seeing and talking to them for hours was the best gift anyone could have given her, she was so happy. And she was grateful and full of energy. The energy you get when you sleep your full eight hours and you get your cup of coffee and continue your day full of errands, and you just know everything is okay. And all your thoughts, problems, and worries for the future are still there, but you have the strength and will that you will end up overcoming them because you just believe you will.

Life continues no matter what

Lolla opened her eyes, and a tear came down her left temple. She couldn't feel her entire body, but she knew she was alive. She was staring at the ceiling, thinking of what happened and wondered what the time was. She heard the whispered mantras from her teacher's mouth, and she tried to reach for Patty's hand. Patty grabbed her hand back and whispered, "Did you see him again?" Patty impatiently asked. Her eyes were wide open, and she had a huge smile on her face.

"I did. And I also saw my grandparents. Patty I had a full dinner with them!" Lolla whispered back and started to cry even more. "They were there – real and just as I remembered them."

"Are you for real? How is this possible, Lolla? I don't believe you." Patty turned a little towards her, still holding tight to Lolla's hand."These dreams of yours are getting really bizarre. Can you tell me how you are doing this, I want to see my uncle," Patty smiled.

"You better believe me. Also, tomorrow after school you are going to teach me how to ride my bike, Colin deserves it," Lolla said and turned her body towards Patty.

"Yes, ma'am! Anything for Mr. Colin! But you have to trust me this time, no helmet included!" Patty whispered and made a funny face. They both laughed and laid back to continue the relaxation.

Lolla closed her eyes and tried to remember the dream. Was it a dream? There was no doubt something extraordinary was happening to her, and she knew it is all happening for a reason. She was a dreamer, a believer, someone who will always find the good in everything, in everyone. Or she used to be, until exactly a year ago. Time has changed her in so many ways since then. She remembered she used to sit on the little red chair at night, in front of her mirror in her room and just look at herself. Her eyes were sad, her mouth was relaxed and the inner feeling of continuing this day was gone. The same picture was repeating over and over before bed. She would look at the pictures, she would remember the moments of happiness, the places, the music, and the life.

The class was over. Lolla opened her eyes and realized this was in the past. Why? Because he has come back and he had brought so much joy to her and her life. There was nothing left to be sad about. Lolla smiled. "Ask, Believe, Receive," she read out loud.

"This is exactly what I was reading." Patty jumped out of her mat and started dancing.

"Haha, I am sure you did, you little funny creature." Lolla smiled and started dancing with her as well.

They left the building and decided to go for some pizza. Right around the corner, there was this little Italian place Colin and she used to go before movies. They sat on a table right next to the window and ordered their favorite pizza – Hawaiian! Lolla remembered how Colin used to make fun of her saying how this is not a real pizza. "How could you put any fruit on a pizza?!" he would always joke about this.

Lolla took a little piece of it and put it on the corner of her plate.

"You are not going to eat that?" Patty lifted her eyebrows in surprise and sipped her Sprite.

"Nope. This is Colin's piece!" Lolla smiled and winked at Patty.

They both knew how funny this would be if he was right there sitting with them and they laughed. And he was there with them for sure, no doubt about that.

Lolla couldn't wait for next Thursday.

There were some chocolate cake and books

Lolla closed the book on her lap and rested her eyes. She would always reread the same books because she believed that every time she reads over a book, she finds something new in the book. People are not always ready for some stuff, and if you are not there yet in your mind and body, it stays hidden for you until the right time and the right moment. So when she was younger, she would decide if a book will be a favorite and will keep rereading it. And she was right – every single time she will be surprised to find a certain detail that would make so much sense with the story. And she never got tired of that.

Lolla was always interested in the self-development section. She would always say how magnificent the mind is and how we can control our reality by making a habit of thinking positively. But not just that – we have to take action, always. There is so much to be learned ,and there is so much also to be discovered, it is endless.

Lately, she had abandoned the power of the mind and was thinking of a more negative way than anything else. How could anyone be positive after losing love? Time was different.

She felt this was also changing, she was waking up every morning and started to say her little prayer of Gratitude, as she called it. Just a simple moment of happiness and appreciating all she was and all she has. Her grandmom taught her this when she was just a tiny three-year-old and used to remind her always that if she does this every morning, her day will be full of joy and blessings. When you are that young and you love your grandmom, this was like a law to Lolla. Something she would always remember from her angel.

Lolla got up from her bed and reached for her phone, she remembered that Patty told her about a charity event she was going tonight. It was late afternoon, and she had no plans, so she decided to join Patty. And it was going to be at the Local Animal Shelter, meaning cute animals everywhere. Maybe her mom would like to join as well if she wasn't busy of course.

She changed her clothes and ran downstairs. The smell of a freshly baked cake filled the whole house, and it was delicious.

"Hey mommy, do you want to join Patty and me at the Animal shelter event tonight?" Lolla smiled and opened the oven. "Mmm, this smells heavenly."

"Wow, you surprise me more and more with every single day now, honey! I have to finish some little work I have left, and then I am all yours." Diana smiled and hugged her daughter.

"Okay, perfect! You finish whatever you need, and I will be right here waiting for you, eating that cake!" Lolla did a little funny dance and opened the oven again.

"Your wish is my command!" Diana smiled. She took her cup of coffee with her and left to the office.

Lolla sat on the bar stool and smelled the cake; it was chocolate – her favorite. Her mom was an excellent baker, and she would always create the best cakes! She put a big piece in her plate and cut a smaller one out of it. She left it on the side of the plate, "Colin, I got you!" she smiled.

Diana sat on the desk, opened her laptop and stared at her face in the desktop. She noticed that her mouth was curved into a little smile. Her heart was happy. There was so much change in Lolla's behavior, and she was very curious about what the reason might be. After months of isolation and no conversations, no urge to live and so many sleepless nights, it seemed like in two weeks things just changed. Was there someone new or was it the yoga class? She decided that tonight was the perfect opportunity to talk to Patty and maybe find out what was really happening.

"Mom, come'on! We have a half an hour to get ready and go! Patty will be here any second now." Lolla's voice shook her out of her thoughts.

Diana realized that she didn't even turn on her laptop,but at least she had the best idea coming to her mind. Diana smiled. There was nothing better than seeing your child getting better from a heartbreak. She felt gratitude, and her entire body shivered.

Is it really Spencer?

atty, Lolla, and Diana walked into the Animal Shelter and felt the spirit of love. So many people were attending, and they could feel the wonderful atmosphere. The shelter was decorated and there was so much food around. People were talking and walking around looking at the animals for adoption.

Patty has been attending this charity every year. She had a husky of her own called Blaze, which she got three years ago from this same shelter. She was always trying to help them and donate all she could save from her job - a true animal lover.

Diana sat on a little green chair and sipped her drink. She remembered the times when she was younger. Her sister once brought a little cat that she found on the street. It was a cold winter, Diana remembered and laughed. They hid the kitty for two days straight from their parents. The kitten was one of a kind and lived with them for fourteen years. She wanted another cat, but her and Martin never got to talk about it. Years passed by and it just never happened. Diana took another sip of her drink and smiled; she was really happy to be here with her daughter. She couldn't wait to tell Martin.

"Mom!" she heard Lolla's voice.

"Yes, sweety, what's up? Are you enjoying yourself here? Everything is beautiful!" Diana answered and continued sipping on her chilled Chardonnay.

"Yes! But, I have to show you something, please mom!" Lolla was trying to hold her mom's hand and Diana could see the excitement that was flowing out of her daughter's eyes.

"I am coming. I am coming; my goodness Lolla!" Diana was trying to follow her daughter through the crowd.

"Mom, meet Spencer!" Lolla was holding this little poppy all black and white, sniggling in Lolla's arms.

"Hey Spencer, nice to meet you, buddy!" Diana started to scratch him behind the ears and realized that more people are coming towards them to take a look at the puppy.

Spencer was only a month old golden retriever,and it was the sweetest baby ever. He seemed to instantly loved Lolla and was almost falling asleep in her hands.

"Mom!" Lolla looked at her mom, and Diana knew.

"Yep, I know, he is the one. You are going to take him out and feed him and do whatever you have to do. Also, you are telling your dad about him."

"Omg, omg!"Lolla was so happy and she started to kiss Spencer and doing a little dance with him.

Diana was looking at her daughter, and her eyes start to tear. She was so happy to see her daughter smiling again. It has been so long. And now she wanted to take care of another being which was absolutely unbelievable. A couple of weeks ago, she didn't even want to take care of herself. Hope seemed to be so far, and seeing her now was the biggest gift for Diana.

"Wow, I knew this is coming up," Diana said, that is why you invited me, you tricky little person.

"Not at all, mom, I had no intentions to adopt any animal. I only came to donate. But when I saw him, I recognized these eyes, they were big and soft,and I knew he has a good heart, he picked me."

They filled out all of the papers and were ready to leave when one of the workers approached them and said, "Ladies, thank you so much for adopting the little guy. You will love him, he has been the sweetest here, I am sure he will bring so much joy to your home. And before I forget, feel free to rename him."

"To rename him?" Lolla asked surprised. But I love Spencer.

"Yes, you can totally leave it then," the man said, but most people like to rename them, especially since they are still so little.

Lolla thought for a second and continued, "No, but thank you! Spencer is perfect!" Lolla smiled.

"Just to let you know, when he was born, one of the nurses called him Colin at first, but this got changed since there was another Colin in here already."

Lolla and Diana stared at the man and then to each other. It was more than obvious – his name was going to be Colin.

Lolla couldn't wait to tell her dad. And to tell Colin as well. There was so much she wanted to share with him; oh if she could just be with him all the time.

Colin was jumping around her feet, and she knew this was meant to be, his tiny tale was moving so fast as he was trying to make a barking sound. *He is just the tiniest and cutest little creature*, Lolla thought. "I will make your life amazing and I promise to take care of you like you are my son!" Lolla smiled.

The event was almost over; people were walking around smiling and enjoying the wonderful evening. Little kids were running around, speaking loud and laughing. The sweets and the soda were showing its effect. A family of three were on a side – the mom was holding a little kitty cat, seemed like it was no more than five-six weeks old. The little girl was softly scratching the baby behind the ears. The dad was looking at them with a huge smile. The charity seemed really successful, and Patty couldn't hold her excitement.

"Guys, this was awesome! I am so happy we end up coming and look at this little soul, he found a home!"

"I know," Diana said, "it seems like a lot of animals got adopted tonight."

"Yes! And they collected a lot of donations, so my heart is full!" Patty smiled and made a heart with her hands.

Thoughts

olla sat on her bed and took a deep breath. Her mind was racing, and she was feeling all kinds of emotions at the same time. There was happiness for sure, so much to be looking forward to. Now she had a little doggy to take care of, and she felt a little scared. What if one morning she wakes up and she feels that horrible feeling of sadness and emptiness, she was so used to them for all these months. They became a part of her; they were her. She couldn't afford this; there was no way. For herself and Colin. And for her family.

She got up and walked to her window and opened it. The backyard was so quiet and empty. It looked like those fancy Persian rugs, all made in bright orange and red shades. She remembered the time when she would wake up from some noise coming from the back yard. She would open her eyes and know that this is Colin, standing under her window, throwing small rocks. It would be so late, and her parents would never let her leave at this time. And she wouldn't pickup her phone because she would always be asleep. So Colin would always walk to her house and make sure she is good and safe. She opened the window and took another deep breath. It has been so long since then, a whole lot of forever.

She heard someone scratching on her left foot and looked down. Colin has woken up and was ready to play. And again, right there next to her window, she had her Colin again, this time even closer to her body. She picked him up and hugged him, and he snuggled in her hair and made a little sound of happiness. Lolla closed the window and went back to her bed, she put Colin by her pillow and put the blanket over him. He was just like a real baby, he closed his eyes, and in a minute he was already snoring.

Lolla looked at her bookshelf across the room; she got it as a gift from Colin for her Birthday, he built it for her. "Your room is a mess, these books are all over the floor, and you keep losing them," he would always say. This was one of the most special gifts she ever got from anyone; it had so much thought in it. She smiled. The bookshelf was all covered in dust; it has been a while since she last organized it or read anything from there. She wiped the dust with her hand and made a decision to clean that whole corner tomorrow. But only if she had some free time after playing with Colin all day. She smiled and even laughed out loud. She used to always laugh at her own jokes.

Colin moved and stretched his legs under the blanket. Lolla walked over the shelf and picked a book. *This will be my night,* she thought, *nothing better than a great book.* She looked around and held her head – everything was reminding her of him, but for the first time this was not bringing her sadness but love. So much love. She felt gratitude and pride for knowing him and for being able to experience him. And she promised herself to never forget that. Colin moved again and turned his head towards her. In his eyes she read, "Are you coming yet, I need a cuddle buddy." Lolla put on her favorite pajamas, laid down on her bed and opened the book. This was for sure one of the best days for the past couple of months. Many deep breaths taken, many promises have been made, and a lot of gratitude was felt.

How to manage a
bicycle ride?

She could see the sun, making its way through the purple shades in her room. Colin was laying down by the bed and instantly jumped up when he felt her waking up. Lolla smiled when she saw him. Mornings used to be her favorite time of the day, everything is fresh, and you can start over.

The smell of something so delicious was coming from downstairs, and she smiled. The book she was reading the night before was still on her bed, open on the page where she fell asleep. She got up and reached for her robe; it was starting to get chilly, and she couldn't wait to get her comfy clothes on.

"Lolla, I hear you, come on downstairs," she heard her mom.

"Coming mom, and Good morning!" Lolla replied. "Just give me a second, I need to wash my face.

"I have a surprise for you, sweety, be fast!"

Lolla grabbed Colin and went down the stairs. Patty was sitting on the high top chair smiling.

"A-ha! I see what my surprise is, mom." Lolla ran to hug her friend.

"I have been patiently waiting for you to wake up, missy," Patty said. "And also patiently waiting to give a huge hug to this amazing puppy."She grabbed Colin out of Lolla's hands and started to dance with him.

"You get ready; we are going to ride bicycles," Patty smiled, "it is time, my love."

Lolla felt the chills running through her body, an instant feeling of fear and excitement at the same time.

"Really, Omg!" Lolla started to jump up and down."I can't wait!"

Breakfast was delicious, and coffee was even better. Lolla and Patty left the house and got into Patty's car. The two bicycles were attached to the back of her car.

Patty drove to the Somerset Park, the weather was beautiful, and it seemed like a lot of people were out enjoying the day. They parked the car and took their bicycles. Lolla took a deep breath and said to herself, "This is it."

The bicycle alley was wide and open, Lolla was walking and holding on to her ride when Patty said, "It's time, my love, let's give it a shot."

"Alright, alright," Lolla smiled and tried to go on the seat.

"Now, try to keep your body straight and start pushing the pedals. Do not look down, look only ahead of you."

"Fine,Pat, Jeez," Lolla was smiling and trying to hold on to the bicycle.

She managed to sit on the seat and looked ahead. She imagined herself as a little girl, back then when she thought she could do anything and it just did not happen. *Not this time*, she thought to herself.

Lolla started to ride the bicycle, and it seemed like someone was holding to her and giving her strength. For a second, she thought that maybe Patty put those extra wheels for little girls on both sides and now she has no trouble riding it. No, it wasn't that, she could feel it. She was riding the bicycle and she was feeling so happy and so free. Patty was looking at her with her mouth open. *This girl is a liar; she definitely can ride a bicycle*, Patty thought.

They spent the whole afternoon in the park, it was amazing. Lolla had so much fun and now she could say she can honestly ride a bike with no problem. If only Colin could see her. Wait, he probably sees her and he also already knew what was going to happen this afternoon.

The afternoon

Lolla came home running. She was so excited to tell her mom about today. She opened the door, removed her shoes quickly, and ran into the kitchen. Diana was not there, but she could smell the fresh baked chocolate cake. Lolla smiled. *This day is turning to be even better*, she thought.

"Mom? Where are you?"

"I am upstairs, honey. You can eat it, that is fine." Diana was laughing.

"Ha ha, will do but I wanna tell you about today, I rode a bike!" Lolla was so excited.

"Really? Coming down in a sec, let me just put my robe on. I took a little nap after work today."

They sat on the counter and cut the cake. Lolla was so happy and excited, and Diana could feel the energy. This was the greatest gift she could receive now, her daughter all happy and healthy, coming back to her normal life, somehow.

"And I have no idea how this happened, I went on the bike and just started riding it, it was really easy. Like something or someone was helping me keep my balance." Lolla was explaining with her eyes and hands. "I thought Patty did something to the bike, but no...."

"Wow! Sweety, this is fantastic." Diana stood up and went to pour herself a glass of Merlot. "I am so proud of you!"

"I think I will do this more often now; I should not let this bike rust. I will definitely give it more love from now on."

They both laughed and enjoyed the chocolate cake. She sun was going down, and the kitchen was looking so pretty with the sunlight coming through the shades. Lolla was looking so beautiful and calm. Everything was coming to its place.

Another date tonight

Lolla heard the alarm and instantly smiled. It was Thursday. She grabbed her phone and dialed Patty, but she did not pick up. The room was really dark and she could hear the rain outside. For some reason, this made her even happier. She never liked the rain before; it would always make her feel alone, but not today.

Her plan for today was already done, she was going to another date tonight at the yoga class. Colin was sleeping on the little rug she had by her bed, and she could hear his little snore. He was growing so fast, and soon he will probably reach ten pounds. The vet was always so happy and polite and was saying how Colin was his favorite. She opened her phone and checked the next vet appointment. He was still a puppy and needed much care and love.

She got up from the bed and tried not to wake him up, but the second she put her feet on the ground, Colin opened his eyes and jumped on her. They started cuddling and fighting, he was getting so big and strong, but he was the sweetest. He brought so much happiness into her life, it was unbelievable.

"Let's eat, buddy!" She kissed his ear and he knew it is time for a snack. He jumped back on the floor and disappeared down the stairs in no time.

Patty called her back and they arranged the whole evening. A movie after class and a walk by the water in the park. Lolla was happy. She went to take a shower, and it was time to decide what to wear for tonight.

The lights were dimmed,and the room was looking more beautiful than ever. Lolla was lying down on her mat and she felt she was out of breath. This was the moment she was waiting the whole day and literally the entire week, and the feeling was unbelievable. She was hearing the meditation music and was trying to relax and close her eyes. Her heart was beating fast, and she smiled. She was about to see and hug Colin again. Patty was lying right next to her, and she could hear her breathing as well. The yoga teacher started reading a beautiful part of a book. Everything became light.

Lolla felt that warmth feeling in her feet and knew she was about to go.

The rain was back. Lolla could hear and feel it. She opened her eyes and found herself standing at a street light, dressed in her yoga clothes. It was freezing and quiet. Everyone around her was frozen, the time has stopped. She was standing by people, ready to cross the street but no one was moving. The child's face was frozen with a smile and was not moving. The cars were stopped, the people in stores and restaurants looked like statues. Only the rain was going strong. She looked around and could not recognize what town or country she was standing in. Her bare feet were freezing, and she looked to hide somewhere. There was a bus stop really close, and she went underneath and sat on the bench. "Where was Colin and what is going on?" She heard a bus coming from a distance, and she went on the street to see it. She saw the lights getting bigger and stepped back from the street. The bus was almost there; it was coming really slow, she could see it was a big green bus and for what she was able to recognize, no one was driving it. The bus stopped right in front of her, and the doors opened. Lolla thought for a second but decided to go in. Her feet were freezing, her clothes were wet, and water was coming down her face and hair. She sat on one of the front seats by the window and tried to hug her legs. The doors closed and the bus continued. She was alone. The bus ride was long. She could see the town, everything was dark, no movement anywhere. There were only statues of people, paralyzed in their lives. It was so quiet, so sad. The bus was not stopping at any of the stops, and she wondered if things were going to get better. She felt scared and confused and was thinking how to wake up from this. And where was Colin?

Lolla put her head on the glass and felt the tears coming down her face. Something was terribly wrong, and she had no explanation for that. Did she do something wrong? Everything she wanted and desired was supposed to be in this moment, seeing Colin again brought her back to life, and she was able to continue her life. It was no fair. She closed her eyes and tried to take a breath, the deepest breath she could ever take.

The bus slowed down, and she opened her eyes slowly. The rain was gone and the sun was coming up, the night was gone too. She thought for a second if she had felt asleep and how long she was out. She felt the exhaustion and her body was aching. The bus stopped and the doors opened. Lolla got up really slow and walked to the door. She looked over at the driver's seat and saw no one. She went down the bus stairs and heard the doors closing behind her bag. The bus continued and soon disappeared from her sight. Lolla looked around and realized that she was at the same spot where the bus picked her up last night. The stop was the same, the people waiting to cross the street were still there, and the smile on the kid's face was still the same. She saw a little boutique and decided to go and see if she can borrow some clothes. The door was opened,and she entered a beautiful store. There were two girls laughing behind the counter and a little girl sitting on a big green chair on a side. Everyone was frozen. Lolla looked around and grabbed a pair of pants and a sweater and changed her clothes. The dry clothes felt so comfy and warm. She said, "Thank you," and smiled at the laughing girls.

Lolla left the store and started walking to the bakery across the street. She wondered how long she would have to stay here, what was this place, what was the whole point and where was Colin? The bakery was small and everyone inside was enjoying the bread and cookies. She smelled the fresh baked cake and thought this was so strange. She grabbed a couple of the baked goodies from the counter and ate them.

They were the most delicious cookies she ever tried in her life. She quietly said, "Thank you, Tamara" to the lady behind the counter and left.

"Lolla!" She heard Colin's voice.

She turned her head to the left and saw him. He was sitting on a bench and was holding a cup of coffee.

"Your coffee, my lady!" he smiled.

Lolla burst into tears and ran to him. She hugged him so tightly and could not hold her tears. Her voice was not coming out.

"Colin! What is this, what is happening? I am so scared!" she cried.

"Hey, don't cry! Please," he said. "This is something you had to go through. Alone."

"I don't understand. I came to see you, to be with you," she replied. "You were not here, I was alone for hours, everyone's life is stopped and why is that. What is this place?"

Lolla had so many questions.She was sipping from her coffee and was trying to calm down, but it was so hard for her.Colin was so relaxed, he was hugging and kissing her.

"Listen, babe. This is life. Everyone's life. We go through it like it is a game. Ups and downs are always rotating, and we have to manage to survive. Last night was your big down, just the same moment when I left the real world and you had to go through it. A bus ride alone in the rain. Exactly how it all feels."

"It did. The sadness was insane. I felt like I was in a dark circle and hope was so far," Lolla said.

"Exactly," Colin smiled. "But you have to understand that it is all needed. You will go back now and continue your life stronger than ever. And will have a wonderful life. And remember, I will always be there with you. Always."

"What do you mean? I don't want to go anywhere, this is my life, here, with you." Lolla felt her tears coming back. She could not lose him again.

"No, babe, this is our last date. I came to show you that you can continue, you are much stronger than you think and I am so proud of you."

Lolla hugged him tightly and they kissed. She felt an enormous feeling of love and gratitude. She felt peace, finally. They looked at each other's eyes and smiled. She was ready.

She has never been more ready. She felt warm and happy, and nothing was left from the horrible night she went through. She sipped her last coffee and closed her eyes.

The meditation music was still going on, and she felt herself laying on her mat. She opened her eyes fast and smiled. Nothing has changed in this real world but in her own world, everything was different. She finally said Goodbye to Colin. She got up and sat on her mat. There was her cup of coffee right next to her left foot. Lolla smiled.